Dedicated to
the "Silver Fox," Donna Rae,
my wife and best friend.
D.L.C.

To my sisters, Kris and Karla, their love,
and encouragement over the years
has been a precious gift.
K.S.G.

Story Copyright © 1995 by Donald Cripe

Illustrations copyright © 1995 by Karen S. Gruntman

Inquiries should be addressed to
Bud's Publishing
101 North Winter Avenue
Goshen, IN 46526

ISBN 0-9649625-0-0
Printed by Mason Printing
106 North Beech Road
Osceola, IN 46561

The Lonely Christmas Tree

by Donald Cripe

illustrated by Karen S. Gruntman

This is a story about a little Christmas tree that lived in a large Christmas tree forest. The other trees called him "Little Tim" because he wasn't like all the other trees in the forest. He was smaller than the others, with fewer branches and a crooked trunk. Because of his appearance the other trees made fun of him and were always teasing him.

It really didn't upset Little Tim that the other trees teased him because he kept thinking that someday he would end up in some nice family's home on Christmas morning. He would have tinsel, lights, and presents under his small thin branches. This had always been his dream and he wanted so much for his dream to come true.

One winter day several men came into the
forest and started cutting down trees that would
be shipped out to be sold for Christmas. Little
Tim was one of the trees cut down and he was
very happy. He was loaded onto a truck and
began his journey.

He ended up at a little white house which was the home of Mr. Jake. He had sold Christmas trees every year for as long as people in town could remember.

During the summer months Mr. Jake could be seen riding his motor scooter around town with a whistle hanging around his neck.

He loved to blow his whistle. He was a strange little man, but people just loved him.

A couple of weeks before Christmas people in town started buying trees.

All the trees around Little Tim were sold. Two days before Christmas Little Tim was the only tree remaining.

He had never felt so sad or lonely before.

On the day before Christmas Michael and Elisabeth went for a walk. Because their parents had been sick and had not worked for several months there would be no money to buy a Christmas tree and presents this year.

During their walk they passed Mr. Jake's house.
Michael and Elisabeth both saw Little Tim at the
same time and immediately fell in love with him.

To them, Little Tim was the prettiest tree they
had ever seen.

Mr. Jake saw them looking at Little Tim and went outside to talk with them.

When Mr. Jake learned that they had no tree, he gave them Little Tim to take home.

They were so happy and excited that tears rolled down their cheeks.

As soon as Michael and Elisabeth left with Little Tim, Mr. Jake got on his scooter and started riding through town, blowing his whistle very loudly.

People came out of their homes to find out what all the noise was about. Mr. Jake told them that Michael and Elisabeth were not going to have any presents under the tree on Christmas morning.

All the people in town gathered together. They
purchased toys and presents for the family.

They also bought lights and tinsel for Little Tim.

When Michael and Elisabeth got up early Christmas morning, they saw Little Tim all dressed up with tinsel and lights on his branches and presents underneath. You could not tell that Little Tim had a crooked trunk and fewer branches.

The children   were so excited they started
jumping up and down.

When Little Tim saw how excited Michael and
Elisabeth were, he said to himself...

"At last my dream has come true."